COMET

THE UNSTOPPABLE REINDEER

by JIM BENTON

For Griffin and Summer

Special thanks to
Kristen LeClerc, Kelsey Skea, Merideth Mulroney,
Deron Bennett, and Emma Reh.

Published by Two Lions, New York
www.apub.com
Amazon, the Amazon logo, and Two Lions are
trademarks of Amazon.com, Inc., or its affiliates.

ISBN-13: 9781542043472
ISBN-10: 1542043476

The illustrations were created using ink and watercolor.

Book design by AndWorld Design
Printed in China

First Edition

1 3 5 7 9 10 8 6 4 2

two lions

'Twas the night before Christmas,
a tense situation.
The elves had worked the whole year
without a vacation.

They weren't jolly or cheery.
They were tired and cranky.
There was some pushing and shoving
between Stinky and Stanky.

And so Comet stepped in
(he hated elf fights).
Then a wild punch connected
and turned out his lights.

When Comet came to
they were all getting along,
but his arm had a bend
where one didn't belong.

The doctor came over
and got to work fast.
He outfitted Comet
with a sling and a cast.

As Comet jumped up,
Doc said with a frown,
You're not going anywhere.
Just sit yourself down.

"No dashing, no dancing,
your arm, it needs fixin'.
It will be a long time
before you're prancing with Vixen."

Later that night
Comet watched Santa get ready.
(His spot had been filled by
a rookie named Freddy.)

"But Comet's the best,"
Dasher whispered to Blitzen.
"I mean, Freddy is nice,
but I'm not sure he fits in."

"I fit in," said Freddy.
"I *so* qualify.
I don't need a degree.
I'm a reindeer. I fly."

Santa hugged Comet
and told him goodbye.
Comet sighed as he watched
them fly into the sky.

It's so very quiet
when the elves all go home
and you're a busted-up reindeer
at the North Pole alone.

Your friends have all gone
to leave good girls and boys
a present from Santa's
great big bag of toys. . . .

"HIS BIG BAG OF TOYS???"
Comet started to yell.
"How could they forget?"
And he called Santa's cell.

But Santa was laughing
at Freddy's bad singing.
With those loud Ho ho ho's,
no one heard the phone ringing.

There was only one thing
that a reindeer could do
to make sure that those toys
got to me and to you.

One single thought
went through Comet's head:
"Always lift with your legs."
That's what everyone said.

With a heave and a ho,
he lifted that bag.
But the weight was so great
that he started to sag.

He tried with a lever.
He tried with a hoist.
He tried till his forehead
was reddened and moist.

"I simply can't do it.
This bag weighs too much.
There are too many toys,
and candy and such.

"I gave it a try.
I can't do any better."
But as he gave up,
he noticed a letter. . . .

"Dear Santa," it said.
Most start out that way.
Or "Dear Mr. Claus," or
"Yo, Tubby—hey."

But this said, "Dear Santa,
It'd be great if you could
bring a toy for my sister.
She's so sweet and good.

"She's too small to write,
but I know what she'd like:
a little green pig
on a little pink bike.

"But there are so many kids,
and the world is so big.
She'll understand
if you can't bring the pig.

"She won't cry a bit.
She won't even pout.
Just don't wear yourself
or your poor reindeer out."

Comet was stunned.
No child, no elf
had EVER put
reindeer ahead of himself.

"But if you can swing it
(it's all up to you),
our house is bright yellow.
The roof is bright blue."

Comet looked at that bag.
It was simply too big.
But at the tippiest top
was that little green pig.

He huffed and he wheezed
and he let out a whine.
Comet felt something slip
out of place in his spine.

But he hefted that bag
like a brave little fighter.
"Would it kill kids to ask
for some toys that are lighter?"

He limped to the map
and looked to the east.
"It's morning there first,"
groaned the belabored beast.

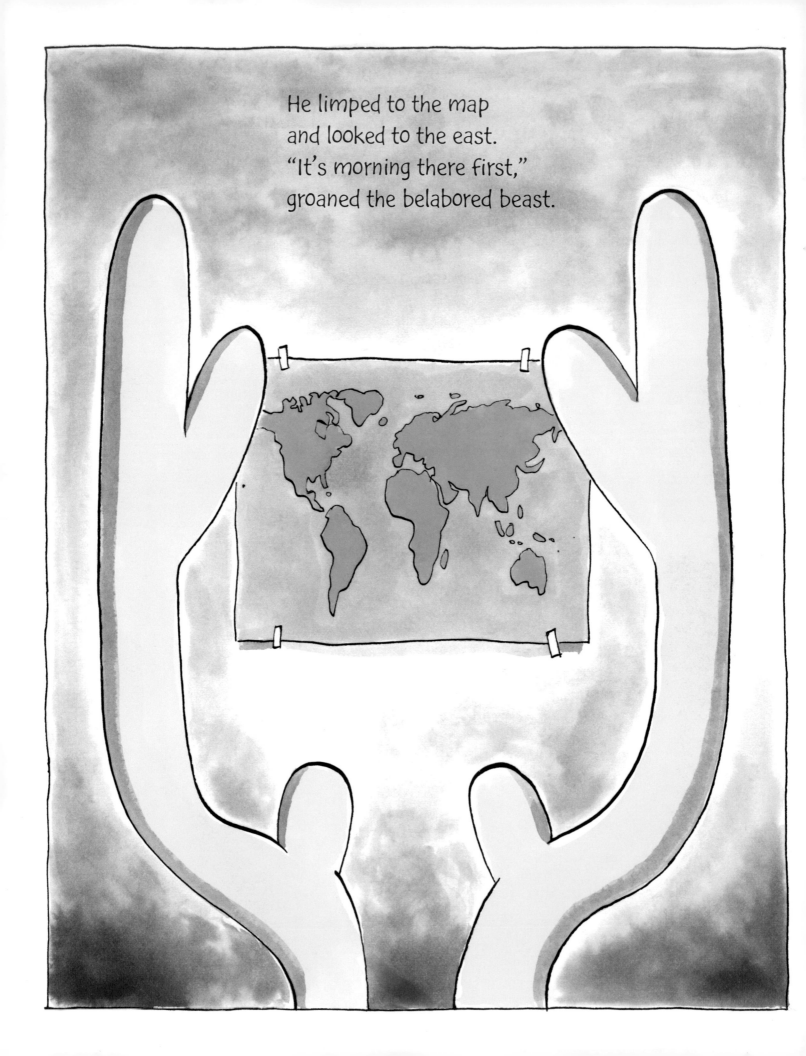

He lumbered outside
and prepared to depart
when he heard the soft sound
of a hernia start.

"I'll begin in the east
and work my way west,"
Comet said as he winced
at a pain in his chest.

He flew to Siberia,
Japan, and New Guinea,
where he knocked out a tooth
crashing into a chimney.

He rested a minute;
he felt kind of queasy.
Santa had always
made steering look easy.

On to Egypt and Sweden,
Italy and France,
where he scraped up his butt
('cause he didn't wear pants).

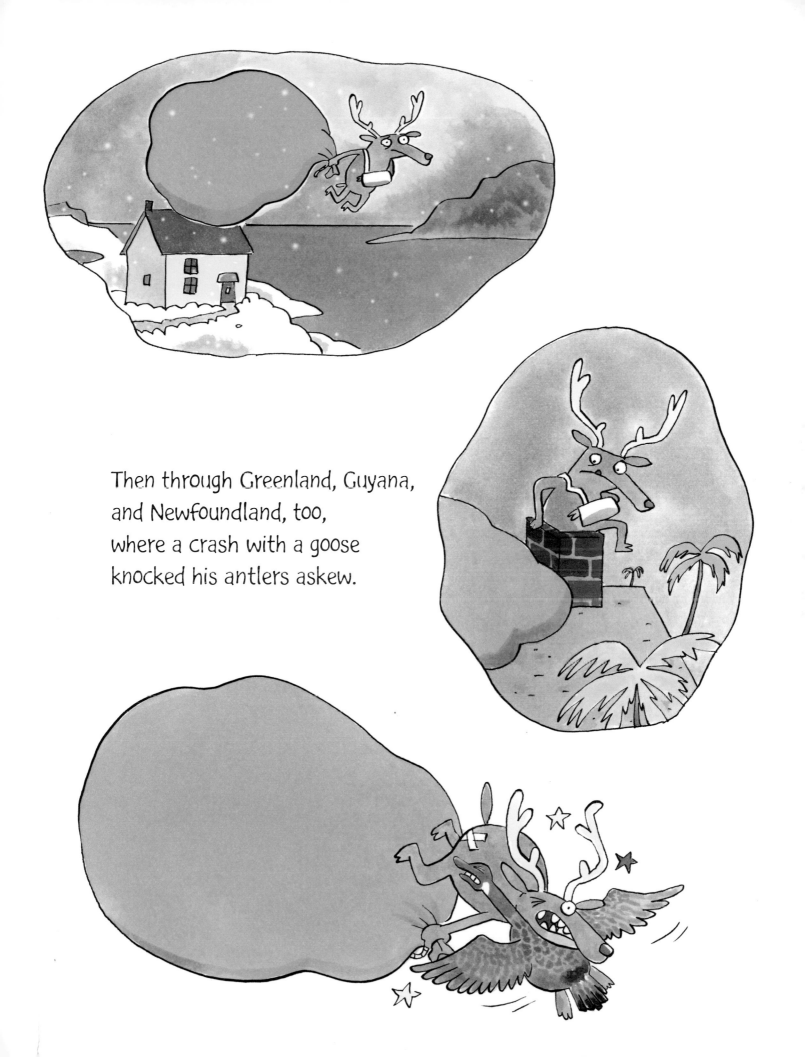

Then through Greenland, Guyana,
and Newfoundland, too,
where a crash with a goose
knocked his antlers askew.

Cleveland, Chicago,
then up to Quebec.
He picked up a limp
and a pain in the neck.

He had left lots of toys
(like a billion or two),
but he'd found no yellow house
with a roof of bright blue.

The night was half-done;
things weren't going so well.
And a lump on his ear
was starting to swell.

He looked in LA.
He looked in Seattle.
Then he borrowed some Band-Aids
from a small herd of cattle.

He flew up to Alaska
through each little town.
But the bag was near empty,
so he sat himself down.

"I've circled the world
and given a toy
to every good girl
and every good boy."

He looked at his map
as he shed a small tear.
"No little green pig
for little sister this year."

That tiny tear fell on
a spot in the Pacific.
Honolulu, Hawaii,
to be more specific.

A surge of delight
arose in his chest
as he plotted a course
that was south by southwest.

Way out at sea,
near the end of his race,
a whale blew his nose
right in Comet's face.

That was all he could take;
Comet felt he was through.
But just then Hawaii
came into his view.

At long last he found
that roof of bright blue
on the house painted yellow
in warm Oahu.

He slipped down the chimney
with a gift for the boy,
and of course, for his sister,
the little pig toy.

He was met by the boy
who had written the letter.
"Gee, your arm's in a sling.
I hope it gets better."

Comet smiled and sighed.
The kid's phone gave a jingle.
"I'll get it," said Comet.
"I'll bet it's Kris Kringle."

It was Santa, of course,
full of thank-yous and praise,
so quick-thinking Comet
mentioned getting a raise.

"And a vacation," said Santa.
"Can the elves have one too?"
asked Comet, who knew that's
the right thing to do.

"We'll all go!" laughed Santa.
"That should heal that bone!"
"Oh, and next time," said Comet,
"please turn up your phone."